JEREMY STRONG once worked in a bakery, putting the jam into three thousand doughnuts every night. Now he puts the jam in stories instead, which he finds much more exciting. At the age of three, he fell out of a first-floor bedroom window and landed on his head. His mother says that this damaged him for the rest of his life and refuses to take any responsibility. He loves writing stories because he says it is 'the only time you alone have complete control and can make anything happen'. His ambition is to make you laugh (or at least snuffle). Jeremy Strong lives near Bath with his wife, Gillie, four cats and a flying cow.

ARE YOU FEELING SILLY ENOUGH TO READ MORE?

LAUGH YOUR SOCKS OFF WITH

JEREMY STRONG

CARTOON KID

ILLUSTRATED BY
STEVE MAY

PUFFIN

PUFFIN BOOKS

Published by the Penguin Group
Penguin Books Ltd, 80 Strand, London WC2R 0RL, England
Penguin Group (USA) Inc., 375 Hudson Street, New York, New York 10014, USA
Penguin Group (Canada), 90 Eglinton Avenue East, Suite 700, Toronto, Ontario, Canada M4P 2Y3
(a division of Pearson Penguin Canada Inc.)
Penguin Ireland, 25 St Stephen's Green, Dublin 2, Ireland (a division of Penguin Books Ltd)
Penguin Group (Australia), 250 Camberwell Road, Camberwell, Victoria 3124, Australia
(a division of Pearson Australia Group Pty Ltd)
Penguin Books India Pvt Ltd, 11 Community Centre, Panchsheel Park, New Delhi – 110 017, India
Penguin Group (NZ), 67 Apollo Drive, Rosedale, North Shore 0632, New Zealand
(a division of Pearson New Zealand Ltd)
Penguin Books (South Africa) (Pty) Ltd, 24 Sturdee Avenue, Rosebank, Johannesburg 2196, South Africa

Penguin Books Ltd, Registered Offices: 80 Strand, London WC2R 0RL, England

puffinbooks.com

First published 2011
008

Text copyright © Jeremy Strong, 2011
Illustrations copyright © Steve May, 2011
All rights reserved

The moral right of the author and illustrator has been asserted

Set in Baskerville
Made and printed in Great Britain by Clays Ltd, St Ives plc

British Library Cataloguing in Publication Data
A CIP catalogue record for this book is available from the British Library

ISBN: 978-0-141-33476-9

www.greenpenguin.co.uk

For Arthur — undiscovered genius.
With many thanks for
the friendship, the letters,
the company and, of course,
the elephants.

Here's
what's
inside!

CONTENTS

This is the noise my brain makes when it can't think:

blurble-
blurble

SPLOOP!

DURRR! KLUNKK!

Now it was the first day back at school and the first day in my new class and the first day with my new teacher. What a lot of firsts. And my new teacher had just asked me a question. WHY ME? Why couldn't he ask someone else? It was a really, really, REALLY difficult question too. First day in class with all these people listening and I don't even know half of them, and my new teacher has to ask me a REALLY difficult question.

That's NOT FAIR!

And do you know what Mr Horrible Hairy Face Teacher asked me? I will tell you.

WHAT IS YOUR NAME?

AAARRGH!

How am I supposed to know THAT?! And
my brain was doing that stupid durrrrrrr
sploop blurble klunkkk thing because everyone
was looking at me. And my eyeballs probably
rolled up inside my head because that is what it
felt like and then . . .

I fell off my chair.

BANG-KERRASH!

And everyone laughed. Mr Nasty
Horrible Big Nose Hairy Face came
across and helped me up and asked
if I was all right. So I said yes and
got back on my chair. Then he
asked if I knew who I was yet and

I said of course I did. Casper. Casper Jenkinson.

Mr Horrible Hairy Face said he had never taught anyone called Casper before. I very, VERY nearly told him that I had never had a teacher called Mr Horrible Hairy Face before. But I didn't, because I am NOT stupid. (Except when my brain goes

DURRR! SPLOOP! blurble KLUNKK!)

Anyhow, I think everyone's brain was doing something like mine because my new teacher pointed to the girl sitting opposite me and asked her what her name was and she just stared at him. He had to ask her again and you'll never guess what she said.

That's not a name. It's a date! At least she didn't fall off her chair like Mr Stupido (ME)!

Mr Horrible Hairy Face didn't laugh. He just smiled and asked her if that was when her birthday was and you know what? IT WAS! That Mr Horrible Hairy Face was pretty clever to work that one out. She went as red as a bowl of tomato soup and said it *was* her birthday and her name was Mia.

Mia has got curly hair that wiggles all over

her head and a turned-up nose and some freckles. She smells of soap so I guess she's got one of those mums that are always saying things like 'Don't forget to wash your hands before you go out'. Don't forget to brush your face and wash your teeth and wear clean underpants and all that rubbish. Except girls don't wear underpants, they have knickers. (Snigger snigger.)

PANTS

KNICKERS

My mum never says anything like that to me. I guess that's why I don't smell of soap.

After that we all said our names and birthdays and Mr Horrible Hairy Face smiled and showed his teeth a lot. He's got an awful lot of teeth and I think he likes flashing them about. Anyway, it turned out he wasn't called Mr Horrible Hairy Face at all, his name was Mr Butternut. (But I think I might still call him Mr Horrible Hairy Face sometimes, like when he's in a BAD MOOD. I know he has bad moods

sometimes, and so do you, because all teachers
have bad moods. You know what they're like.)

YACK YACK
YACK SILLY BOY YACK
YACK YOU'VE DONE IT ALL
WRONG YACK
YACK YACK.

Well, Mr Butternut looked at us all for a
long time and we all looked back at him with
big, round eyes. Then he went over to the old
armchair in the corner of the classroom and
sat down. You can tell it's old because the
stuffing is coming out of one arm. I think the

class hamster got hungry and ate it.
My friend Pete's got a
hamster called Betty.
She's always escaping
and eating the carpet and cushions. I've
got a chameleon called Colin. He's very
exotic and changes colour but he
doesn't eat the furniture, only insects.

Yum yum!

Mr Horrible Hairy Face told us to
come and sit around him, so we did.
Then he told us to sit closer, so we
shuffled together, and he said we still
weren't close enough. Well! If I got any
closer to Mia I would have been sitting

on her lap and I was NOT going to get as
close as THAT.

Mr Butternut leaned forward. He bent down to us and he spoke very softly like this:

'This is your first day with me and I can see that there is something amazing about you. You may not know this but all of you are hiding a BIG SECRET. I am the only person who knows what your secret is and this is what I know. You are all . . .'

And we all fell over backwards because he shouted so loudly. I can tell you, it made us all feel very excited to know that we were superheroes.

Mr Butternut said that if we believed in ourselves we could do ANYTHING. I'm not so sure about that because of course we can't do ANYTHING. For starters, we can't blow up the school without getting into BIG TROUBLE.

(BAD IDEA)

And I'm hopeless at maths, unlike Sarah Sitterbout, who is on my table and is probably the cleverest girl in the world and knows EVERYTHING. I think she probably eats brains for breakfast. She can spell 'silhouette' AND SHE KNOWS WHAT IT MEANS!

WOULD YOU LIKE ANOTHER BRAIN, DEAR?

She knows her seven times table and she once wrote a story that was eight pages long and it wasn't even in big writing.

When we got back to our table I sat there wondering what kind of superheroes we might

VACUUM GIRL

MR BIGMOUTH

be. I LOVE drawing. I do it all the
time. I can't stop myself. You should
see my school books. They're covered
in doodles. Anyhow, superheroes are
very good at Doing Things. I couldn't
think of anything I was good at, except
drawing, of course – and falling off my
chair. Plus I am short and thin and have
knobbly knees and ginger
hair. Pete calls me

BALLOON BOY

ZAP!

The Ginger Twiglet and Stick Insect and stuff like that. I call him Penguin Pete and Big Nose and stuff like that. We are BEST friends.

So I drew a picture of my friend Pete. He sits next to me and has been my friend ALL MY LIFELONG LIFE. He isn't good at anything either, but he does have a big nose and big ears and very big feet.

When I say 'big'
I mean they are
MASSIVE – as
big as skateboards!

Huh! That's
nothing. You
should see
what MY
eyes can do!

Pete looked at my picture and his

eyes almost popped out of his head. He

does that when he's excited. His eyes

bulge until you think they're going to go

SPING! right out of his head.

'Why have you drawn me with great

big feet and a huge nose?'

'Because you've GOT great big feet

and a huge nose.'

'They're not THAT big,' he

complained. 'You've made me look like

a giant penguin.'

And that was it – BRAINWAVE! I got
REALLY excited. I'd found my first superhero!

'Pete! It's you, as a superhero. Big Feet Pete!'

Then Pete got very excited and hit me on
the head with his reading book and said I
should be called Massive Ginger Twit Person.

'Because you *are* ginger. And you're a twit.
I look as much like a superhero as a hamster in
a tutu.'

(In case you don't know what
a tutu is, it's one of those frilly
skirts that ballerinas wear and it's
supposed to make you look like a
fairy, but I think it just makes you
look STUPIDO!! Especially if you
happen to be a hamster.)

SARAH SITTERBOUT'S BIT ABOUT TUTUS

Tutus were first worn by ballet dancers in about 1880. There are different types but the most famous tutu is one that sticks straight out and is often called the pancake tutu. I like pancakes a lot, especially with honey or jam. I put jam on my pancake tutu once and my ballet teacher was NOT very happy.

'Anyhow,' said Pete, 'I'm going to call you Cartoon Kid because: (1) you are always drawing comicky stuff and (2) you're an idiot.'

I said thank you very much and I told Pete very calmly that he was the nicest person I had ever met. So we hit each other a few times and after that we started looking around the classroom to see what other superheroes we could invent. And do you want to know something? There were lots.

They are meant to be superheroes? Don't make me laugh!

It's very difficult saying ANYTHING with a tongue like mine.

For starters there was Lucy, who wears glasses and has a brace on her teeth and says 'yeth' instead of 'yes' and 'thothageth' instead of 'sausages'. It's not her fault. She can't help it and one day she'll say 'sausages' properly, just like that, and we shall all clap because she's been trying hard for a long time.

Mr Butternut says we all have things we can do and things we can't do and none of us can be good at EVERYTHING. Except, of course, for Sarah Sitterbout. Pete asked Mr Butternut what he wasn't good at and he turned very red and wouldn't tell us, so it must be something like he doesn't eat his food tidily.

Anyhow, we decided to call Lucy the Mighty Munch, because of her teeth, which are a bit noticeable.

'And Mia has to be Curly-Wurly-Girly,' said

Pete, which made me laugh.

'That's great!'

Mia doesn't like her curls and comes to school wearing a big hat, but her hair still sticks out. It looks like she's wearing a hat full of spaghetti, probably all the spaghetti Mr Butternut has dropped on the floor. Pete thinks Mia is very pretty and he likes her, especially as she plays football and is a brilliant goalie. BUT she's still a GIRL, isn't she? Huh.

So, who else is there? There's Sarah Sitterbout, of course. She's as smart as an entire space station full of computers and stuff and she makes me mad because she knows EVERYTHING

'Oooh, Pete's in love with Mia!'

before anyone else does.

At break time I said that Sarah's superhero name should be Big Brain.

'But she's fat and her bottom sticks out,'
Pete argued. 'You can't be a superhero if your
bottom sticks out.'

'Why not?'

'Because,' he said.

'Because what?'

'Because because. Has Superman got a
giant bum? No. We should
call her Big Bum, not
Big Brain.'

'But Sarah is
very clever,' I
pointed out.

'OK,' he said.
'How about we
call her Big Bum Brain?'

And we laughed like monkeys in a
chocolate-banana shop. Then we talked about
some of the others in class.

'What about Noella Niblet?' asked Pete.
'She's always whining about something. I know
– the Massive Moan?'

I grabbed Pete's arm and creased up
laughing. 'No, I've got the best one ever. The
Incredible Sulk!'

'Brilliant!' cried Pete. 'And there's Hartley Tartly-Green. He's so stuck-up, just like his mum and dad. He's such a snot-box.'

'Bang on,' I grinned. 'Snot-box is PERFECTO.'

We were laughing and sharing my packet of crisps when who should come along but Murder on Legs. Also known as the Vampire Twins – Gory and Tory.

They are in an older class and are therefore BIGGER. Also, they always wear black and their faces are very white.

They have pointy boots that look as if they could stab you and pointy steel fangs too. (They don't really, but they definitely look like vampires and I'm sure their teeth are a bit longer every time I see them.)

POINTY FANGS!

POINTY BOOTS!

Gory and Tory loomed right over us, casting a vast, gloomy shadow like the Cloud of Death. Everything suddenly went very cold. We tried not to show how scared we were. Unfortunately, nobody had told my knees about not being scared and they started knocking together all by themselves. (I have got the skinniest legs EVER and VERY knobbly knees.)

There may be trouble ahead . . .

'Those are our crisps,' said Tory, while her sister picked at her fangs. (She was probably

KNOBBLY KNEES

picking out bits of the
last child she'd eaten.)

'No, they're mine,'
I said. 'That's why
they're in my hand.'

'You stole them
from our bag,' said
Gory.

'No way!' I blurted.

'We're not even in
your class,' Pete said.
He could have run
away, but he didn't.
Now you know why
he's my very best,
bestest friend.

'I saw you steal them,' said Tory. 'You took them from our bag. Give us those crisps.'

The Vampire Twins made a grab for the crisps but I was too quick. *FWOOOOOOSH!* Pete and I were speeding away across the playground like lightning on Rollerblades.

The Vampire Twins came thundering after us, screaming horribly, with their coats flapping like giant bat wings.

'Help!' I squeaked. (You know how your voice goes when you're scared? It doesn't work properly, does it?)

'Do something!' yelled Pete. So, of course, my brain sprung into supersonic action and went:

DURRR! SPLOOP! blurble blurble PLOP KLUNKK!

And then, P-ZING! It came to me.

'Come on, you know what Mr Butternut said – we're superheroes!' I yelled. 'We must fight back!'

So we skidded to a halt, spun round and almost melted with terror because the Vampire Twins were nearly upon us. Pete gripped my arm fiercely.

'Come on, let's do it. Let's . . .

PLEASE TURN
OVER!

But it wasn't quite like that . . .

'I'll take those crisps, thank you so much,'
Tory sneered, plucking the bag from my hand.

'And now we're going to pizzarize you both,'
snarled Gory.

I gulped. My brain was going *durrrr sploop
burble.* HELPPP! What could we do to escape?

'You go that way!' Pete yelled at me.

He dived to the left so I went to the right.
The Vampire Twins tried to get both of us and
crashed into each other head on.

We made our escape and hid round the corner, panting like monkeys in a lion enclosure.

'We did it!' Pete grinned.

'Yeah, but we lost the crisps,' I moaned.

'They're here,' said a little voice. It was Mia! She'd rescued our crisps!

'I jumped in the air and caught them while they were giving each other a big headache,' she explained. 'I don't think they even saw me.'

'You are so amazing!' said Pete.

The three of us went and sat on a bench, sharing the crisps.

'I thought you were very brave,' Mia told us.

I was brave once. I looked at myself in the mirror without scaring myself to bits.

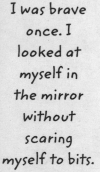

Pete nodded wisely. 'The thing is, when you're facing Death like that, you've just gotta do what you gotta do.'

I stared at my best friend. What on earth was he talking about? He hadn't done anything. He'd run away, just like me! Before I could think of an answer Pete was passing the bag of crisps to Mia.

'Have some more,' he said, looking at her adoringly.

Yuck, I'm going to be sick.

This is the noise I make when I discover something horrible, like my big sis, Abbie, has got a brand-new spot on her face and it's as

big as Australia. It looks pretty volcanic

too. It will probably explode soon

and her head will turn into a huge

eruption.

It's also the noise that comes

out when Mum wants me to

help her make a cake in

the kitchen, which means

DEATH BY BOREDOM.

Mum is ALWAYS baking cakes.

She makes them for birthdays
and weddings. But she is super-
dooper-splooper when it comes
to decorating them. My
mum can make a cake look
like ANYTHING you like. But
it's very boring helping her. I'm just
her slave and all I ever get to do is stir
things for years and years. AND she
never lets me lick the spoon.

But this time it was nothing to do with my big sis or Mum. It was Colin, my chameleon. He had

DISAPPEARED. It was Abbie's fault. She had found a dead fly and decided to feed it to him. Unfortunately she left the lid loose on his tank!

Huh! That sister of mine is a big diddly-dozy brain, if you ask me. She just does not THINK. Well, she does sometimes but it's always the same. She only thinks about face cream, hair, lipstick and BOYS. I bet her brain is stuffed full of them and nothing else.

I'm over
here!

Anyhow, I went to see Colin and he
was – gone! I raced round the house like
my pants were on fire.

'He's gone! Colin's vanished!'

'Oh dear,' smirked Abbie. 'Has your
only friend in the whole wide world
packed his suitcase and left you all
alone? I'm not surprised.'

I could feel my face turning into
a red-hot radish. 'Colin is NOT my
only friend. There's Pete and . . .' My
mind went blank. Who else was there?
'Anyhow, it was YOUR FAULT.'

Dad looked up from the TV. 'Abbie, that's rather unfair. You could at least apologize.'

'Apologize?' squawked Abbie. 'To a ginger biscuit?'

'I AM NOT A GINGER BISCUIT!'

'Abbie!' snapped Dad. 'Now you can apologize for the loose lid AND for calling Casper names.'

Abbie's eyes narrowed to tiny slits. I knew what that meant. It meant she was dreaming up umpteen different ways of killing me. Well, no probs, because I was thinking up umpteen different ways of killing HER.

Abbie muttered 'Sorry' through gritted teeth and stamped off to her bedroom.

Result! I felt pretty pleased. I had a sun-sized grin on my face, which was a lot better than an Australia-sized spot, I can tell you.

Dad turned to me. 'Actually, Casper, your room is in such a mess it's no wonder you can't find Colin. He's probably sitting on top of that mountain of smelly clothes on your floor, looking like a dirty sock. Go and tidy your room and you'll probably find him. And don't forget it's your mother's birthday tomorrow,' he shouted after me.

Mum's birthday? Already? How old was she this time? Mum had been twenty-nine ever since I'd known her. And what about a present? I was as skint as a hippo. (Well, have you ever known a hippopotamus with a bank account?)

Typical. Just when I thought I was winning I get sent off to tidy my room AND I have to think of something to give Mum for her birthday. Huh.

BRRRINNGG!

Hooray! Saved by the bell – the doorbell. It

was my big pal Pete from next door.

You see, Pete's parents split up three years ago and now his mum has got this massively dull boyfriend. His real name is Derek.

'You can call me Uncle Derek if you like,' he told Pete when they first met. And he gave Pete a big, cheerful smile that showed his goofy teeth, not to mention the gap where one was missing. He wears brown suits and big, flappy ties. That Uncle Derek is about as interesting as a plate of liver and onions.

So whenever Uncle Boring comes round, Pete usually escapes to our house. 'Cos your parents are cool,' he told me. Well, that was news to me. I'd always thought of them as being lukewarm. Anyhow, I had important news for my pal and I told him about Colin's great escape.

I'm not escaping. I'm going for a walk.

Pete shook his head sadly. 'I know how you feel. My hamster Betty is always escaping. Don't worry,' Pete announced, 'we'll go on a chameleon hunt! We'll need food, a tent and a telescope to spot elephants.'

'There aren't any elephants,' I told him, puzzled.

'That's because they're still in Africa and that's why we need the telescope.'

'But it would take the elephants ages to get here from Africa,' I pointed out.

'Not if they catch the bus,' Pete said.

'Which bus?'

'The number 53,' Pete answered.

I thought for a moment and grinned. 'Anyhow, the elephants won't be a problem. All we have to do is turn the telescope round and look through the wrong end. Then the elephants will look teeny weeny tiny. Like ants.'

'Brilliant!' cried Pete. 'I'm definitely not scared of elephant ants.' He clasped me on the shoulder. 'You do realize that you are a Grade One Ginger Twit Person, don't you?'

Now, here's a weird thing – when Pete calls me names, I don't mind. I guess it's because we're best friends. (If it had been Abbie calling me names, or anyone else, I would have boiled

over, like Mum's jam did once. What
a mess! It looked as if a mega-gigantic
strawberry had exploded on top of the
stove.)

JAM BOILING
OVER

CASPER
BOILING OVER

I'm behind
you!

I grinned back at Pete. 'We need
some food. Let's raid the kitchen. Keep
an eye out for Colin the Chameleon.'

'Not to mention the elephants,' added Pete.

On the way to the kitchen I told Pete about Mum's birthday and he suggested I should make something.

'Like I should knit her a sock or something?'

'Only if you want her other foot to get cold. It would have to be at least two socks.'

'How about three socks?' I suggested.

Pete shook his head. 'You mustn't spoil her,' he said as he started searching the kitchen cupboards for food. Suddenly he got very excited and his eyes went springy. Pete's eyes are really bulgy, especially when he's excited. He grabbed my shoulders and started shaking me.

'Totally fantastic idea coming! It's getting bigger and bigger. I can feel it in my head. It's like a ginormous glittery balloon in there, all shiny and new and amazing!'

'Pete, just say what it is, will you?' (He was still shaking me.)

'Right. It's not one thing – it's TWO for the price of ONE!' cried Pete. 'You know we've got that homework to do for Horrible Hairy Face?'

'Yeah. Make something. That's all he said. Pretty boring.'

'I agree, but why don't we make your mum a birthday cake? So at the same

time we will also be making our homework!
See?'

Actually it was a pretty neat idea. Two jobs
done in one. You see, Pete isn't totally stupid,
he's totally *brilliantly* stupid.

'OK, I admit it's a good idea.' I said. What
kind of birthday cake shall we make?'

Pete pulled a large bag of flour from the
cupboard.

'A cakey-kind of cake, of course! It could even say "HAPPY BIRTHDAY, MUM!" on it,' he raved. 'It would be a brilliant surprise. She's always making cakes, but now *you* will be making – for her!'

I thought about it. My parents had gone to the supermarket. Abbie was in her room with her friend Shashi, which probably meant they were putting on make-up and talking about boys. We had the kitchen to ourselves.

Pete looked at me, his eyes still jumping with excitement.

'You must know how to make cakes. Your mum does it all the time and you help her.'

I thought about that too. Hmmm. Yes. Pete was right. I did know.

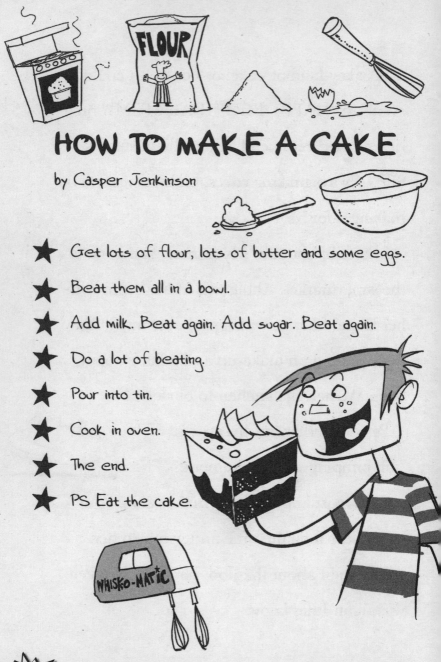

HOW TO MAKE A CAKE

by Casper Jenkinson

★ Get lots of flour, lots of butter and some eggs.

★ Beat them all in a bowl.

★ Add milk. Beat again. Add sugar. Beat again.

★ Do a lot of beating.

★ Pour into tin.

★ Cook in oven.

★ The end.

★ PS Eat the cake.

'There's icing too,' I added.

'Yeah, we'll do that bit when we get to it,' Pete said confidently.

Mum's big mixer was already set up on the side. I got a box of eggs and some milk from the fridge. Pete tipped in the flour.

'Is that enough?' he asked.

'Not sure,' I said, and he tipped in some more. 'Still not sure.'

So just to be certain we put in the whole bag. I started on the eggs. Those eggs were the wibbly-wobbliest eggs I have EVER come across. They rolled everywhere. Eggs are such a useless shape. Why can't they be square or oblong?

I managed to drop the first one on the floor, and the second one fell out of its shell before I could even get it into the bowl.

'You're a knobbly-kneed nincompoop,' said Pete. 'Let me do it.' He put the last four eggs into the bowl and hit them with a rolling pin until they broke open. 'See? That's what you do.'

'But now there are bits of eggshell in there.
How do we get them out?'

'You're so fussy. Lots of animals eat
eggshells. Dogs, pigs – '

'Pete, I'm not a pog – I mean a dog or a pig.
I'm a human being. And so is my mum.'

So Pete fished about with his fingers and got out most of the shell. I tipped in a pile of sugar and added the milk. Pete put in the butter.

Put it on LOW. It should be on LOW!!!

'Right-ho,' said Pete. 'Let's go!'

I looked at the settings on the mixer.

'I think Mum always puts it on HIGH,' I said and I switched it on. The machine roared into terrifying life.

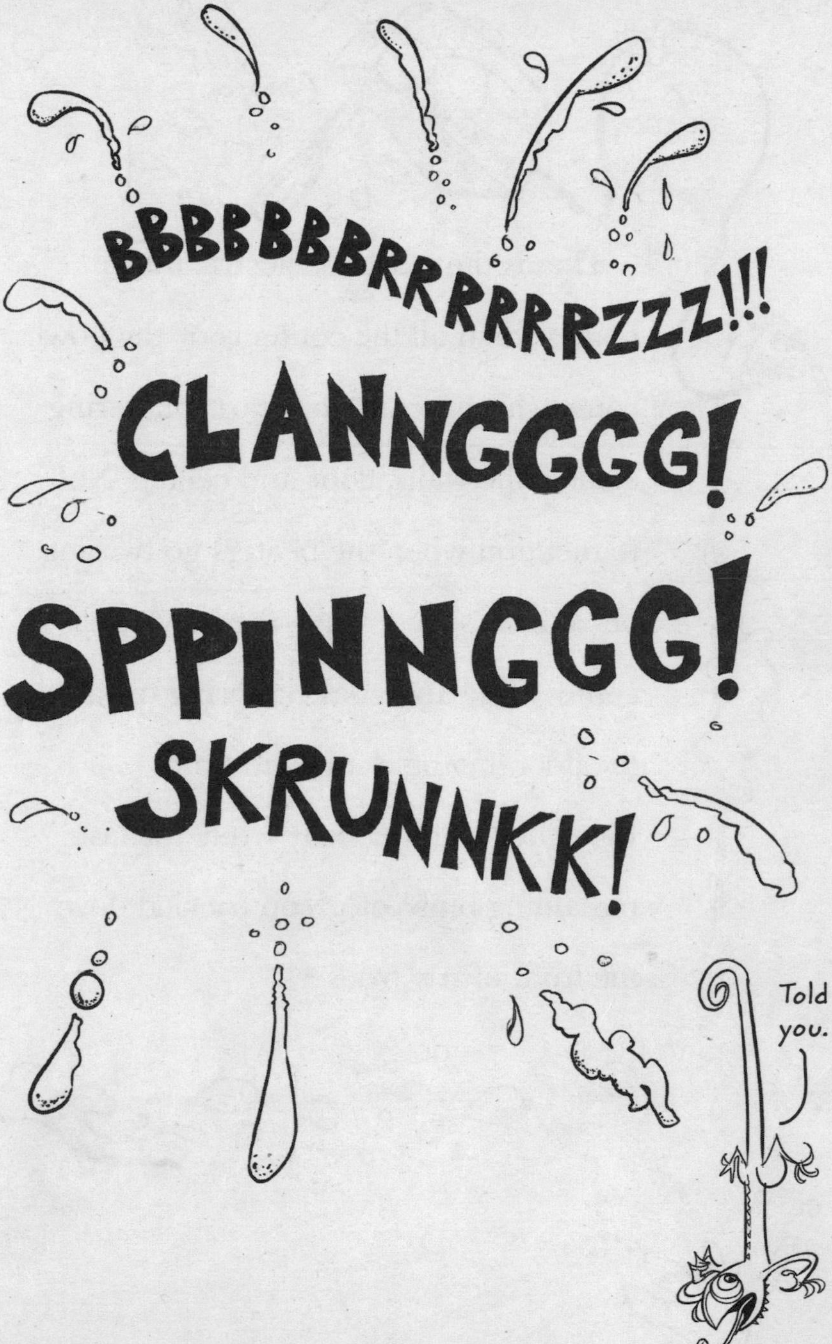
BBBBBBBRRRRRRZZZ!!!
CLANNGGGG!
SPPINNGGG!
SKRUNNKK!
Told you.

That is the noise an electric mixer makes when all the contents of the bowl come whizzing out and start splattering against the walls, floor and ceiling. Not to mention when the beaters go twirling off at high speed, while the bowl itself comes loose and goes clattering towards the floor. I caught it just in time.

I clutched it to my belly while the last remaining blobs of gloop trickled down the front of my trousers.

Pete switched off the mad machine and we stared at each other in horrified silence. And that was when we heard the car pull up outside.

Pete and I went straight into FULL PANIC MODE. 'What are we going to do?' he yelled.

'Only one thing for it,' I shouted back.

Yeeeess. Well, of course we didn't escape and the police elephants, cleverly disguised as Mum and Dad, didn't exactly arrest us, but they didn't exactly congratulate us either. In fact we were in DEEP DOO-DOO. You might have thought my mum would be happy that I was trying to make a cake for her birthday, but she wasn't – no way.

'Whose idea was this?' Mum demanded.

'Mine,' admitted Pete. 'It's meant to be our homework.'

'Home*work*?' cried Mum. 'This is a home-wreck!'

I think she was a little bit upset.

Pete was sent straight home while I was made to clear up every bit of the mess. It took me about sixty gazillion and a half years.

Abbie came downstairs with her friend

Shashi to see what all the noise was about,

and they both stood in the kitchen doorway,

mocking me.

They were still laughing at me when I saw a wasp land on Abbie's cheek. She froze with horror, grabbing Shashi's hand and squeezing it in terror. Abbie began to make a strange squeaky-leaky noise.

'Urrrrrrrrgh, it's a wasp! There's a wasp on me! Save me! Someone stop it! Urrrrrrrrrrrgh!'

And then Shashi started moaning too. 'Abbieeeeeeeeee, you're breaking my hand! Stop squeezing it so hard! Aaaaaargh!'

We all stood there like statues,

wondering what to do. And then guess what?
No, you never will, so I will tell you what
happened next. A long, VERY sticky tongue
shot out of a kitchen cupboard and

SPLURRPPP!

It grabbed the wasp and flicked back into the
cupboard!

Yum yum, wasp
for my tum!

I dashed across, threw open the cupboard door and there was Colin, munching on the wasp and looking VERY pleased with himself. I don't think the wasp was pleased, but at least Colin was happy – and I'd found him!

So the next day was Mum's birthday and all I could give her was a homemade card. It said SORRY in big letters and I had drawn a picture of a birthday cake. Inside there was another drawing. It was a slice of the kind of cake I thought she'd like. I'd cut it out so it looked a bit like a real slice of cake.

At school on Monday Mr Butternut arrived
with a big plaster on his forehead. He asked
everyone to show the class what they had
made over the weekend. One by one we stood
up and displayed our work.

Hartley Tartly-Green (aka Snotbox – ha ha!) had made a model of the Eiffel Tower. It was good, VERY good. In fact it was SO good it had obviously been made by his parents. So that was CHEATING. Typical. Everyone knew, even Mr Butternut, but nobody said ANYTHING because we were all too polite.

Sarah Sitterbout showed us a big stripy knitted square. 'I'm going to make lots of them,' she explained. 'Then you stitch them together to make a rug and you give it to a very old person like Mr Butternut's mum to keep them warm in the winter.'

Mr Butternut told Sarah that actually his
mum was only fifty-seven. Noella Niblet's jaw
almost fell off.

And Mr Butternut burst out laughing,
though I'm not sure why.

Finally Pete and I had to stand up and do
our bit and it was obvious we didn't have
anything to show at all.

The class fell about, all except for Hartley Tartly-Snotbox-Green. 'No, you weren't,' he whined. 'You're making it up!'

'And you didn't make that Eiffel Tower,' Pete shot back. That silenced him!

I looked at Mr Butternut and shrugged. 'So basically the cake got spread all over the place and we couldn't bring it to school.'

Mr Butternut smiled and started

to chuckle. 'What a brilliant excuse, and you've got a story out of it. You've given me a good idea, boys. Let's all write a story about what we made. You can illustrate it too.'

Pete stuck his hand up. 'Mr Butternut, you just said let's write about what WE made, so YOU must have made something too. What did you make?'

Mr Butternut turned pale and he clasped a hand to his head. Suddenly his face brightened. 'Yes, I did make something.

I made a mess of my head by walking into a glass door. I had to go to hospital and I was superglued together again.'

That Mr Butternut is very funny sometimes.
We fell about.

'People don't get superglued,' Mia giggled.

'They do,' said Sarah Sitterbout, who knows
everything.

'It's true,' said Mr Butternut. 'The nurse
used superglue to mend my cut. I felt just like
Humpty Dumpty. And now we're all going to
write.'

And that's what we did – the whole class. Every one of us wrote about what we had made. But Pete's and mine was the best!

BERRANNG!

KLUDDD!!

SKRRASSH!!!

OW-WOW!

This is the noise my class makes when half
of us fall off our chairs, which is what we
had just done. We had toppled over because

WHAM-BAM-Jelly-AND-Jam!

Mr Butternut had just shouted at us. Mr Butternut can shout louder than an earthquake. He was reminding us that we were all superheroes. When Mr Butternut jumps on his chair and shouts like that it makes me feel powerful

enough to do ANYTHING. I could probably

balance the whole world on my head!

Mr Butternut had been telling us about a very special competition in our school. It is called:

THE ETHEL SNUFFLEBOTTOM

COMPETITION FOR THE BEST

CLASS IN THE WHOLE SCHOOL

That is a very long title for one competition, which is why it had to trail down the page like that. I have no idea who Ethel Snufflebottom is.

Whenever my class hear Ethel
Snufflebottom's name they start giggling. Mr
Butternut says my class sounds like a box of
squirrels being tickled. And when he says that
sort of thing, my class giggle EVEN MORE.

Anyhow, Mrs Ethel Snufflebottom (snigger snigger) had given the school a big, REAL silver cup for the competition.

Most competitions are just for one thing, like running or swimming or dancing (yuck-urggh-choke-choke) or maths (aaaargh!) and so on.

But this competition was for EVERYTHING. You could win points for story-writing, art, football, science – even drawing cartoons like I do because I'm Cartoon Kid!

The class with the most points wins the cup, and that means any class can win, even the tiny tiddly toddlers who get points just for tying their shoelaces properly.

Or for going to the toilet before it's TOO LATE! (Which is very embarrassing and happened to me once, but only because Mrs Dinosaur, who was my teacher when I was five, went rabbiting on and on about making sure we asked to go to the toilet in good time. She droned on for so long I wet myself. Mrs Dinosaur was not her real name. It was

DRONE

DRONE

Mrs Dine, but we called her Mrs
Dinosaur because she seemed a bit like
a diplodocus if you squinted your eyes
up tight and then looked at her.)

Pete and I had never been in a winning class but Mr Butternut reckoned we had a good chance this time. That was why he was telling us we were superheroes and we had all done some extra-super-dooper work, even Noella Niblet, otherwise known as The Incredible Sulk (because she moans about EVERYTHING!). However, there was one big problem and that was – well, to put it simply, the problem was Masher McNee and the Monster Mob.

They come from the class above mine and they had never won the trophy either. Masher is built like a bulldozer, behaves like a bulldozer and makes bulldozer-y noises.

Masher and his mob like terrorizing smaller kids and they were out to make sure they won the Ethel Snufflebottom trophy. Strange things were happening round the school. Half the models that the eleven-year-olds had made for Technology disappeared from the display in the hall and were never seen again. Creepy!

Miss Trimm's class of six-year-olds had painted some great portraits of each other. But someone had sneaked into their class when it was empty and drawn moustaches and beards on the faces. Or put arrows through their heads!

'I think Masher McNee and his gang did it,' Mia declared, trying to stop her massive curls getting in her face. She sits at our table and Pete is in love with her. He says he isn't, but he is really.

Pete agreed with Mia. 'We'll have to be careful Masher McNee doesn't try to nobble OUR work.'

'He knows about the stories we wrote,' Mia pointed out. 'Because Mr Butternut read some of them in assembly and your one about the messy cake was really funny. I was laughing so hard my stomach hurt.'

Pete grinned with pride. And I thought, *Just a minute, Pete and I wrote that*

I like stories about flies being eaten.

story TOGETHER! It all happened in MY house!

LET'S TELL MR BUTTERNUT. MAYBE HE CAN THINK OF A PLAN.

THAT'S BRILLIANT. YOU'RE REALLY CLEVER, MIA.

And do you know, MIA BLUSHED!

Good grief! It was so disgusting! I felt as if I was about to be invited to a wedding. And they're only nine! I had to take Pete to one side to warn him. I looked at him VERY SERIOUSLY.

'Pete,' I said, because that's his name, 'Pete, you are too young to get married. You haven't even got your own house yet, or a car.'

Pete looked at *me* VERY SERIOUSLY.

'Casper,' he said, because that's *my* name, 'you are a small, knobbly-kneed twig person and sometimes I think your brain has decided to run away from home and find somewhere else to live, hopefully somewhere sensible.'

Anyhow, that afternoon we had one of the best bits of the competition – the Ethel Snufflebottom Quiz. Each class had a team and ours was Sarah Sitterbout (who knows absolutely EVERYTHING), Hartley Tartly-Green (who *thinks* he knows everything) and me, because I'm quite good at making wild guesses.

We reckoned we had an excellent chance of doing well because Sarah was our

SECRET WEAPON.

She is such a brain box. Her brain is probably as big as a space station. The only thing Sarah Sitterbout is no good at is football.

So we took our places for the quiz and our very first question was difficult.

Even I knew Italy was a country and not a capital city. Sarah looked very upset and wouldn't look at me. She stared glumly at the table. The next question came.

'How does a boa constrictor kill its prey?'

WAS THAT WEIRD OR WHAT?

Sarah Sitterbout was an expert

on animals! I knew that for

sure because she once found

a deadly Black Widow Spider

crawling up my sleeve and she saved

me from it. She picked it up WITH

HER BARE HAND! SHE DIDN'T

EVEN WEAR GLOVES! Sarah said

it wasn't a Black Widow Spider at all.

It was a Cardinal Beetle and she

would call it James.

SARAH SITTERBOUT'S BIT ABOUT SPIDERS AND BEETLES

It's easy. Don't get in a muddle. Spiders have eight legs and beetles have six.

Black Widows are found in warm countries. Cardinal Beetles are red and pretty. There are lots of pretty beetles, especially the ladybirds.

Most beetles are very useful because they eat pests like aphids and greenfly.

I think it would be very good if ladybirds ate people like Masher McNee.

After that it got worse and worse. Sarah either got the answers wrong or said she didn't know the answer at all. We came LAST! I couldn't believe it.

Sarah rushed from the room and wouldn't speak to anyone. I didn't even see her when she left school.

I'm clever. When I grow up I'm going to be Lord of the Flies.

Pete and I walked home together. We have to. We live right next door to each other.

We were almost home when we heard someone crying. They were doing it very quietly, as if they didn't want anyone to hear. We peered over a wall and there was Sarah.

Pete and I looked at each other,

wondering what to do. I bent over the wall,

touched her shoulder and asked her if

anything was the matter.

SOB! 'Everything's the matter,' she sniffed. **SNIFF!**

We went into the garden and sat either side

of her. 'You can tell us,' said Pete helpfully.

'We're your pals.'

'No, I can't. I can't tell anyone.'

'Maybe we can help,' I suggested.

'I doubt it, unless you've got a tank and an

army and everything,' sniffed Sarah.

I chuckled. At least she still had a sense of

humour. I took a gamble. 'I've got two armies,'

I told her. 'They're up my sleevies.'

'And I've got two more,' Pete joined in,

waving his armies like windmills. It should

have made Sarah smile but unfortunately Pete
waved his arms about so wildly he clunked her
head.

'Come on, Sarah, what's the problem?'
I asked.

She took a deep breath. 'Masher McNee has
got Cuggles.'

Pete and I looked at each other blankly.

CUGGLES? IS THAT A DISEASE? DO YOU GO SPOTTY ALL OVER?

'No!' wailed Sarah. 'It's my cuddly fluffy rabbit. I've had him since I was a baby and Masher has kidnapped him. He said if I answered any questions right I'd never see Cuggles again!'

Well! No wonder Sarah bungled the quiz. That Masher McNee had a lot to answer for. Huh. If I ever got my hands on him I'd, I'd – well, actually, I'd probably run a mile. Very fast. I thought the Vampire Twins were Bad

News but that Masher was Bad News stuck on the end of a bomb.

UH-OH!
Pete has
another
idea!

Sarah told us that Masher had the rabbit in his bag and Pete said he had an idea. I groaned. Pete's ideas usually come from the Land of Bonkerdom. But in fact, after he had explained it, the sun came out on Sarah's face and she was a lot happier. We would just have to wait until the next day at school to put Pete's plan into action.

BIG SURPRISE! When Pete and I went into class it was like entering The World of Gloom. Everyone looked totally glum. Noella Niblet, who is a right sulkpot (and a left sulkpot too) and always looks fed up anyway, now looked ten times worse than glum. There was an awful lot of glum in that classroom.

The floor was covered with little scraps of paper.

'It'th our thorieth,' sobbed Lucy, and the insides of her glasses misted up with tears. Pete and I call her The Mighty Munch because she has the biggest brace ever on her teeth. It makes her lisp when she's speaking.

'Thumbody'th hath torn them into little pietheth.'

Pete and I scowled at each other. 'Masher McNee and the Monster Mob!' we chorused.

So then Tyson started wailing as well. Tyson is bigger than me but he is scared of absolutely EVERYTHING. He'd scream if he saw a ▮ tree or a fried egg or a caterpillar. Tyson's superhero name is, guess what? Scaredy Pants! It couldn't be anything else, could it?

So now Lucy and Tyson were both sobbing. I thought we'd all drown in a pool of tears. Luckily Horrible Hairy Face arrived at that moment.

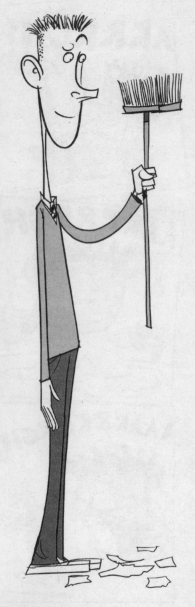

He strode into the classroom, took one look at all the paper on the floor, handed a broom to Cameron and told him to sweep up. Cameron looks a bit like a broom himself because he's tall and thin. He's probably the tallest boy in the school even though he's only nine. He's a bit like the BFG but we call him the BFC instead – Big Friendly Cameron.

We waited for Mr Butternut to say something about the torn-up stories but he went straight to his desk and began to call the register. Didn't he care about our brilliant stories?

I put up my hand. 'Excuse me, Mr Butternut, but those are our stories, all torn up.'

'Are you sure?' asked our teacher. He opened his bag and pulled out a thick wodge of papers. They looked familiar.

OUR STORIES!

Mr Butternut grinned. 'I had a feeling something awful might happen to them. So I photocopied your work and took the originals home for safekeeping, and here they are! It's the copies that got torn up.'

Wow! Did we cheer or what? (We cheered!!) That Mr Butternut is pretty clever if you ask me. (And he's still pretty clever even if you don't.)

VERY CLEVER

Observer book of CAPES

BOOKS R COOL!

So we were very happy about that, but we still had to sort out Masher McNee and rescue Sarah Sitterbout's rabbit, Cuggles.

When break came we went out to the playground. This was it. This was the moment when Pete and I were going to face Masher and his gang.

YIKES!
Only
10p?
I'd charge
£1.00!

We found Masher by the water
fountains. He was charging 10p to
anyone who wanted a drink. The
Monster Mob were there too, looking
very evil.

Pete squared up to Masher. 'You've
got something that doesn't belong to
you.'

'So you'd better hand it over,' I added,
trying to sound really hard.
Unfortunately my voice sounded about
as threatening as a squashed frog. My
heart was going bonkers too. I thought
it would jump right out of my mouth.

Masher whirled round and glared at
us. His face broke into a nasty sneer.

'Oh, look, it's Batman and Robin. Have you come to save the world?'

I watched in horror as the Monster Mob took up a position behind their leader. I mean, there were three more of them and they looked TRIPLE MEAN.

I swallowed hard. 'Hand over the rabbit, Masher. It isn't yours.'

Masher pulled a soppy face. 'Ooooh, diddums wants his wabbit. Ooh, coochy coochy!'

I turned bright red and the Monster Mob burst out laughing. Pete and I weren't getting anywhere. Masher's face suddenly took on a hard scowl and he stepped towards us. Now my heart really DID jump out of my mouth. Not only that, but it ran off, terrified. My legs turned to jelly.

'Go back to Mummy,' Masher growled, and his hands scrunched up into big fat fists.

There was only one thing for it. I looked at Pete. He looked at me. We screamed.

WHAM-BAM-Jelly-and-Jam!

But, of course, it didn't happen quite like that . . . Masher McNee pulled Cuggles from his bag and triumphantly held him up.

'Look what I've got!' he crowed. 'I've got a little rabbit!'

One of Masher's gang giggled. 'What are you going to do with it, boss?'

If you ask me, that Masher McNee is very, VERY BAD.

Pete and I looked at each other. It was time to put Pete's plan into action. Do you know what we did? We really did shout:

He's not just bad - he's mad, bad and UGLY!

WHAM-BAM-Jelly-AND-Jam!

As soon as they heard this shout, THE
WHOLE CLASS came rushing over and
surrounded Masher McNee and the Monster
Mob. THE WHOLE CLASS!!

It was brilliant! Masher could see there
was no way he could win this one. He threw
Cuggles at Sarah and folded his arms crossly.

WE'RE STILL
GOING TO WIN THE
COMPETITION!

But Masher's class didn't win. The final part of the competition was a massive maths test. Guess who came top? Tyson Scaredy Pants! I forgot to tell you he was a cracker at maths, didn't I? So, what with our stories and maths and everything, we won the Ethel Snufflebottom trophy.

HOORAY!

There's something else too. Sarah Sitterbout was so impressed with the way Pete's plan worked out that she's taken a fancy to him, big time! Pete's got TWO girlfriends now.

He doesn't know what to do! Serves him right!

HELP!

So that's how we became superheroes and I hope we stay superheroes forever and ever. After all, Big Feet Pete will need ALL his superpowers if he's going to have TWO girlfriends! (Snigger snigger.)

I fell in love with a chameleon once. I was looking in a mirror.

LAUGH YOUR SOCKS OFF WITH Jeremy STRONG

Jeremy Strong has written SO many books to make you laugh your socks right off. There are the Streaker books and the Famous Bottom books and the Pyjamas books and . . . PHEW!

Welcome to the JEREMY STRONG FAMILY TREE, which shows you all of Jeremy's brilliant books in one easy-to-follow-while-laughing-your-socks-off way!

MY BROTHER'S FAMOUS BOTTOM

Nicholas's baby brother, Cheese, is famous. Well, his bottom is, because he advertises Dumper disposable nappies . . .

JOKE BOOKS
You'll never be stuck for a joke to share again.

THE HUNDRED-MILE-AN-HOUR DOG
Streaker is no ordinary dog; she's a rocket on four legs with a woof attached . . .

COSMIC PYJAMAS
Pyjamas are just pyjamas, right? Not when they're COSMIC PYJAMAS, swooooosh! . . .

Ask Jeremy

Of all the books you have written, which one is your favourite?

I loved writing both **KRAZY KOW SAVES THE WORLD – WELL, ALMOST** and **STUFF**, my first book for teenagers. Both these made me laugh out loud while I was writing and I was pleased with the overall result in each case. I also love writing the stories about Nicholas and his daft family – **MY DAD**, **MY MUM**, **MY BROTHER** and so on.

If you couldn't be a writer what would you be?

Well, I'd be pretty fed up for a start, because writing was the one thing I knew I wanted to do from the age of nine onward. But if I DID have to do something else, I would love to be either an accomplished pianist or an artist of some sort. Music and art have played a big part in my whole life and I would love to be involved in them in some way.

What's the best thing about writing stories?

Oh dear – so many things to say here! Getting paid for making things up is pretty high on the list! It's also something you do on your own, inside your own head – nobody can interfere with that. The only boss you have is yourself. And you are creating something that nobody else has made before you. I also love making my readers laugh and want to read more and more.

**Did you ever have a nightmare teacher?
(And who was your best ever?)**

My nightmare at primary school was Mrs Chappell, long since dead. I knew her secret – she was not actually human. She was a Tyrannosaurus rex in disguise. She taught me for two years when I was in Y5 and Y6, and we didn't like each other at all. My best ever was when I was in Y3 and Y4. Her name was Miss Cox, and she was the one who first encouraged me to write stories. She was brilliant. Sadly, she is long dead too.

When you were a kid you used to play kiss-chase. Did you always do the chasing or did anyone ever chase you?!

I usually did the chasing, but when I got chased, I didn't bother to run very fast! Maybe I shouldn't admit to that! We didn't play kiss-chase at school – it was usually played during holidays. If we had tried playing it at school we would have been in serious trouble. Mind you, I seemed to spend most of my time in trouble of one sort or another, so maybe it wouldn't have mattered that much.

14½ Things You Didn't Know About

Jeremy Strong

* * * * * * * * * * * * * * * * *

1. He loves eating liquorice.

2. He used to like diving. He once dived from the high board and his trunks came off!

3. He used to play electric violin in a rock band called **THE INEDIBLE CHEESE SANDWICH**.

4. He got a 100-metre swimming certificate when he couldn't even swim.

5. When he was five, he sat on a heater and burnt his bottom.

6. Jeremy used to look after a dog that kept eating his underpants. (No – NOT while he was wearing them!)

7. When he was five, he left a basin tap running with the plug in and flooded the bathroom.

8. He can make his ears waggle.

9. He has visited over a thousand schools.

10. He once scored minus ten in an exam! That's ten less than nothing!

11. His hair has gone grey, but his mind hasn't.

12. He'd like to have a pet tiger.

13. He'd like to learn the piano.

14. He has dreadful handwriting.

And a half . . . His favourite hobby is sleeping. He's very good at it.

It all started with a Scarecrow.

Puffin is seventy years old.
Sounds ancient, doesn't it? But Puffin has never been
so lively. We're always on the lookout for the next big
idea, which is how it began all those years ago.

Penguin Books was a big idea from the mind of
a man called Allen Lane, who in 1935 invented
the quality paperback and changed the world.
**And from great Penguins, great Puffins grew,
changing the face of children's books forever.**

The first four Puffin Picture Books were hatched in 1940 and the
first Puffin story book featured a man with broomstick arms called
Worzel Gummidge. In 1967 Kaye Webb, Puffin Editor, started the
Puffin Club, promising to **'make children into readers'.**
She kept that promise and over 200,000 children became
devoted Puffineers through their quarterly instalments of
Puffin Post, which is now back for a new generation.

Many years from now, we hope you'll look back and
remember Puffin with a smile. **No matter what your age
or what you're into, there's a Puffin for everyone.**
The possibilities are endless, but one thing is for sure:
whether it's a picture book or a paperback, a sticker book
or a hardback, **if it's got that little Puffin
on it – it's bound to be good.**